Ella's School Trip

by Jackie Walter and Alex Naidoo

W

FRANKLIN WATTS
LONDON•SYDNEY

Ella had a note in her book bag.
It was about the school trip.

"A trip to the museum,"
said Mum. "You will have fun."

"I don't want to go," said Ella.

"Why not?" said Mum.

"I don't want to go on the bus," said Ella. "Where can I sit?"

"You can sit next to Josh,"
said Mum.

"I don't want to go," said Ella.

"Why not?" said Mum.

"Where can I eat my lunch?"
said Ella.

"Your teacher will tell you where to eat your lunch," said Mum. "You will have fun."

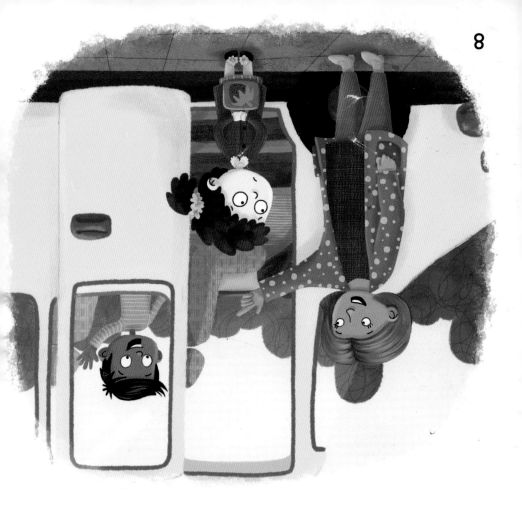

"You can sit next to Josh."

"On you get," said Miss Jenkins.

It was the day of the trip.

Ella sat next to Josh.

They played I Spy all the way
to the museum.

"My gran has a toy like this,"
said Ella. "It must be very old."

The museum had lots of toys.

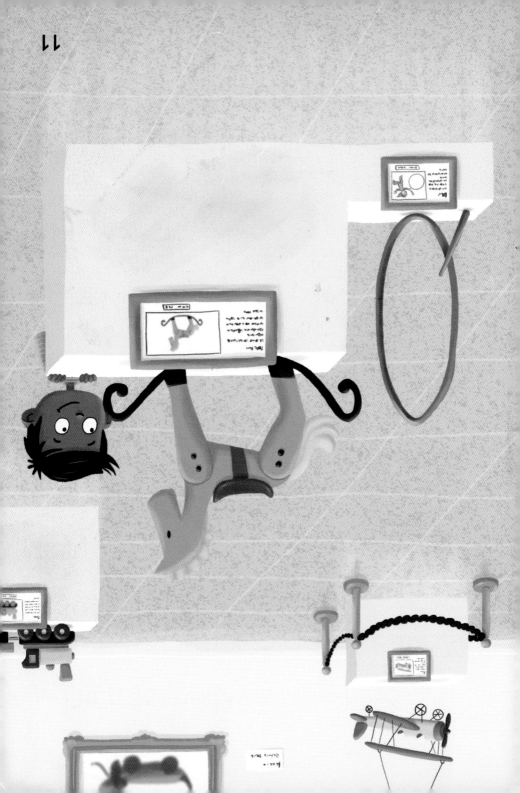

Then Josh saw something.
"My mum has a doll like this,"
he said.

"And my dad has a car
like this," said Ella.

Soon it was time for lunch.

Ella sat next to Josh.

"I like eating in the museum,"

she said.

The bus took the children
back to school.
Ella sat next to Josh again.

Everyone sang songs
and Ella joined in.

Mum was waiting for Ella.

"Did you have fun?" she said.

"Yes," said Ella. "I did!
And so did Josh."

Story trail

Start at the beginning of the story trail. Ask your child to retell the story in their own words, pointing to each picture in turn to recall the sequence of events.

Start

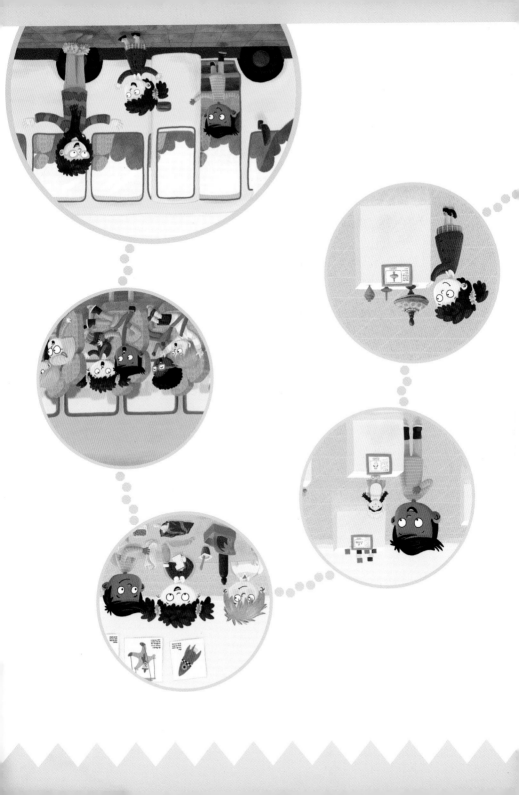

Independent Reading

This series is designed to provide an opportunity for your child to read on their own. These notes are written for you to help your child choose a book and to read it independently.

In school, your child's teacher will often be using reading books which have been banded to support the process of learning to read. Use the book band colour your child is reading in school to help you make a good choice. *Ella's School Trip* is a good choice for children reading at Blue Band in their classroom to read independently.

The aim of independent reading is to read this book with ease, so that your child enjoys the story and relates it to their own experiences.

About the book

When Ella learns that she is going to go on her first school trip to a musuem, she is very nervous. Where will she sit on the coach? Where will she eat lunch? There are so many things to worry about ... but she has forgotten her friend Josh will be there too!

Before reading

Help your child to learn how to make good choices by asking: "Why did you choose this book? Why do you think you will enjoy it?" Look at the cover together and ask: "What do you think the story will be about?" Support your child to think of what they already know about the story context. Read the title aloud and ask: "What is Ella getting ready for?" Remind your child that they can try to sound out the letters to make a word if they get stuck.

Decide together whether your child will read the story independently or read it aloud to you. When books are short, as at Blue Band, your child may wish to do both!

During reading

If reading aloud, support your child if they hesitate or ask for help by telling the word. Remind your child of what they know and what they can do independently.

If reading to themselves, remind your child that they can come and ask for your help if stuck.

After reading

Support comprehension by asking your child to tell you about the story. Use the story trail to encourage your child to retell the story in the right sequence, in their own words.

Give your child a chance to respond to the story: "Did you have a favourite part? Which part was it and why?"

Help your child think about the messages in the book that go beyond the story and ask: "Why do you think Ella was nervous before the trip? How do you feel about doing something new for the first time?"

Extending learning

Help your child understand the story structure by using the same sentence patterns and adding some new elements. "Let's make up a new story about a school play. Ella is nervous. 'What will I wear? Where will I stand? What if I forget my lines?' But her classmates will help her of course! What will happen in your story?"

In the classroom your child's teacher may be reinforcing punctuation. On a few of the pages, check your child can recognise capital letters, full stops and question marks by asking them to point these out. Find the question marks and ask your child to practise the expression they used for asking questions.

Franklin Watts
First published in Great Britain in 2019
by The Watts Publishing Group

Copyright © The Watts Publishing Group 2019

Series Editors: Jackie Hamley and Melanie Palmer
Series Advisors: Dr Sue Bodman and Glen Franklin
Series Designer: Peter Scoulding

A CIP catalogue record for this book is
available from the British Library.

ISBN 978 1 4451 6804 3 (hbk)
ISBN 978 1 4451 6806 7 (pbk)
ISBN 978 1 4451 6805 0 (library ebook)

Printed in China

Franklin Watts
An imprint of
Hachette Children's Group
Part of The Watts Publishing Group
Carmelite House
50 Victoria Embankment
London EC4Y 0DZ

An Hachette UK Company
www.hachette.co.uk

www.franklinwatts.co.uk